The Elephant Hunter

WILLIAM FLAGG MAGEE

Lyrdel A —
A real light in
The dark — you
are a bright shining
star — Bill

Eloquent Books

Eloquent Books
An imprint of Strategic Book Group
P. O. Box 333
Durham, CT 06422
www.StrategicBookGroup.com

ISBN: 978-1-60911-421-3

Printed in the United States of America

Book Design: Judy Maenle

Acknowledgements

The author would like to thank Charlotte Emery for asking to see the rough draft of this manuscript. Her editorial eye and helpful questions were invaluable.

The author is thankful for those who preceded him in this earthly journey, and who have preceded him into Eternal Life: Thyrza Benson, Thyrza Flagg, Montague Flagg, Flora Grace Dean, Walter Magee, Richard Dean Magee, and those all who preceded them. They live on.

A Story of Change:
The Beginning

What one finds at some point is the desire to discover who one really is. People often become defined by their careers, illnesses, marriage(s), or escapades, and in the process of building this exterior facade, their interior life is ignored. One's interior life has to do with who one really is when all the careers, marriages, and escapades have been stripped away and one stands naked—naked within one's own self. St. John called it "naughting one's self," as in stripping away all interior and exterior phoniness.

Authors like Morton Kelsey, Rollo May, and Micrea Elides suggest that by remythologizing one's life, one may discover the reality of who one really is, stripped, standing naked in front of one's self, looking at the real you. This means, according to these men, one lives one's life according to a myth. Rollo May's *A Cry for Myth* was the book Willy read that had had a profound effect. Morton Kelsey was a profound thinker, Episcopalian priest, Jungian analyst, author, lecturer, role model, and Willy's spiritual director, by chance and persistence. His correspondence with Kelsey was the spiritual glue that held him together during an extremely difficult period in his life. Willy hadn't a clue about "naughting," but against good advice he stepped out to experience the shredding of all his self-designed imagery, both interior and exterior. Willy said he thought he could not get back to reality. He later learned that remythologizing was almost as unpleasant as St. John's Dark Night of the Soul. The good news is that the sun rises in the East.

John Benson, his oldest friend, watched as Willy's life was remythologized by the transformation of a relationship that for over half a century had caused untold suffering. What resulted from the suffering was the transformation of two torn, tortured lives. John Benson called it a "gift of God's grace." He told some people the story of Willy's transforming experience and was asked by most of them to put it in writing. This is a story of that transformation.

The End is But the Beginning

Nurses had come and gone, and supper had come and thankfully stayed down. He refused any sedation to help him sleep. He breathed a quiet sigh of relief as the last interruption of the night disappeared. He then fantasized about what might happen when he was set free. He was, at that moment, delusional, and thought himself in another place and time.

Getting up from the bed, he went to a window that overlooked a meadow in a valley in the Great Basin and adjusted the shutters to let the evening's light into his room. He then went to a chair that looked reasonably comfortable and sat in it. He wiggled around to get settled, and when he became settled he sat still with his hands open in his lap. He closed his eyes, took several deep breaths, shook his arms, let his feet flop onto the floor, and began to meditate.

Quietly, breathlessly, he sank deeper into the consciousness of his subconscious mind. Doors opened, windows ushered in soft, cool breezes, and images slowly appeared. Thus begins the story within a story.

Willows

He walked through the willows, hearing the creek ahead of him. He could smell the water. Snaking the fishing pole carefully through the branches blocking his way, he swore silently. The grass was damp, and the dampness worked its way through the soles of his boots. The Prince Albert tobacco can in his hip pocket held the worms. Fish loved worms, and he wanted fish for dinner. When it came to fishing, he was a pragmatist. Friends talked animatedly about the purity of fly-fishing, but they'd never confronted the willows nor, did he think, they would like the slimy feel of a ball of worms as they fell out of the tobacco can. There was a little soil in the can to give the worms a homey feeling, but they always managed to entangle themselves into a slimy ball.

At last he saw the bend in the creek. There watercress and green reeds were growing along the bank. He knew if he let the hook, with worm attached, float under the vegetation, a fish would bite. Running some line off the reel, he held the pole under his right arm and deftly slipped the hook into and down the length of the worm. There was about eighteen inches of line between the sinker and the hook; just right. Transferring the pole into his right hand, he moved several yards above the spot where he hoped to catch a fish. Extending the pole over the creek, the line gently disappeared under the current, and the hook and worm made their way the designated spot. There was a

5

sharp tug. He expertly set the hook and brought the fish ashore. Taking it off the hook, he firmly swatted its head against the heel of his boot and ran the end of a willow branch into the gills and out the fish's mouth. Turning back to the task at hand, the process was repeated several more times. He cleaned the fish. He moved upstream, and getting on his stomach, positioned himself so he could drink the cold, clear water that bubbled up from the springs that fed the steam. It was delicious. Splashing the cold water on his face he used his shirttail as a towel. He sat down and smoked a cigarette.

The fish natives to the creek were speckled, eight to ten inches long. The cold water was home to small fresh water shrimp and other insects making the fish's flesh pink. Rolled in seasoned flour and fried in butter, they were sweet and tender; a delicious meal accompanied by watercress salad and creamed corn. A meal fit for a king.

Walking out of the willows, his mouth watered as he thought of the dinner he would soon enjoy. He put the fish in the back of the pickup and headed home. He came to the road of decomposed granite. It crunched as he made his way toward the small rocky hill just below the Bull Field. The little rocky hill was next to the creek. He parked the pickup short of what his great-aunt called "nigger heads." These were hardened clumps of mud that poked their heads up at unevenly spaced intervals and played hell with whatever wheeled vehicle drove over them. The base of the little hill was covered around the bottom with greasewood and higher up stands of rabbit brush. At the top of the hill were intriguingly arranged granite boulders that he always knew were home to innumerable rattle snakes. Over the years he had never seen any kind of snake, just dried skins left from shedding.

Behind him, the horse pasture drifted away into buck brush that led into a branch of the creek, taking water to the west side of the alfalfa field. Between the creek and the fence and below the buck brush, the ground gave way to salt grass and a landscape crusted with alkali and rabbit brush. He never really liked that part of the ranch. There was an ancient wooden gate that dragged the ground when it needed to be opened, and beyond it lay a vast sea of sagebrush and alkali stretching to the foothills. Beyond them lay the Toyiabe Range extending to the north. On hot summer days when the wind came up on "the flat," dust devils danced across the landscape.

As It Was and Still Is

The pickup headed up the short slope, and he gazed across the pasture. The horses hadn't come down from the big corral, but the cattle grazed along the far fence line. The expensive and quite big Hereford bull stood off to the side, as if standing watch. The bull, her favorite son, was a specimen of genetic perfection. He was descended from Mark Donald on his father's side and an equally well-bred cow. His sons had been busy changing the shape, size, and value of the commercial herd. In short, he was a good investment. The cows liked him. In the distance, snow-topped Mt. Callahan stood in silent approval.

The corrals materialized into view. They were stockade corrals made from juniper posts. His grandfather had built them. The posts were set in trenches, and pipe was wired to the top of the posts to provide support. There was a rectangular barn that had feed bunkers inside one end and six "box" stalls to house thoroughbred horses. The barn was made from adobe bricks. The roof was made of cottonwood poles stretching maybe fifteen feet that rested on vertical poles placed every six feet. Overlaying the cross-timbers were willow branches layered in opposite directions. There were lots of willow at the ranch; many layers of willow branches provided ample support for several layers of decomposed granite that finished the roof. The rain, when it fell, and snow in the

winter provided ample sealant for the decomposed granite, making a solid roof. It was wonderfully cool in the
summer and held heat the horses provided in the depths
of winter. It was used to house horses, bitches in heat,
and bitches with puppies. There were two tack rooms,
one for his father's horses and another at the opposite
end his mother used. He had attempted to redo one of
the stalls as a tack room. It worked quite well.

Pulling in front of the house his grandmother had
built, he went inside and put the fish in the sink. He then
went to feed the horses and fill the water troughs. Dinner cooked and savored, he walked back to the corrals
to see the horses. He liked horses, and to see them as
the sun set over the mountain relaxed him. Returning
to the house, he went into the living room, turned on
some lamps, and settled in to read the book he started
the previous evening. The living room held an elegant
gate-legged table and was surrounded by four antique
straight-back chairs with cane seats. In the center of
the table sat an old painted tray with a sterling silver
sugar bowl and silver salt and pepper shaker. The table
and chairs were in a corner across the room from one
of the two windows, flanking the fireplace. Adjacent to
the table was an old, but quite stately, blue leather couch
with an end table and Chinese porcelain lamp. Sitting
next to the lamp one could look out the window to one's
right or the double doors at the opposite end of the room.
The glass-paned doors opened onto a small flagstone
patio and overlooked Postley Field and Austin Meadow
stretching to the south.

In the center of the room was a Persian rug of pre-
dominately red and blue hues. At opposite ends of the

rug stood small white armchairs, and behind and to the right of the chair nearest the patio door stood an elegant English drop-leaf desk. On the other side of the same chair was a two-cushioned couch. If one sat on the small couch and happened to look up, and knew what to look for, there was a patch in the ceiling, the result of his .410 pump going off due to his attempting to break it down to clean it. When it wouldn't come apart, he pulled the trigger. It made a horrific boom and scared the hell out of Willy, his grandmother, and great-aunt, who thought he'd managed to shoot himself. His father gave him a certificate from the Indoor Shooting Association in honor of hitting the ceiling from the inside the house.

One of the sights always filling and firing his imagination was the early morning sky. Before the sun began to rise, the heavens seemed to be covered from one end to the other with stars and galaxies. It would have been difficult to find a thousand points of light among the millions looking down upon him. Once in a while, a meteorite would cascade across the sky in a fiery arc. He hoped some of it might land in an unpopulated area and be found by hikers or cowboys moving cattle. The times he was up early enough to witness this magnificent spectacle, he wondered how it all came to be; who or what made it, when, how? How was it that he was where he was, and not someone else? Millions of sperm struggling to get to one lonely egg, and out of the millions only one would succeed. Who in the long line of ancestors, current and long dead, would prove to be dominant? What was the composition of genetic pass-through? Why was he having these thoughts? What gave him his consciousness?

Going into the bathroom to shave, he looked into the mirror to see if he recognized who was looking back at him. He tried to imagine what some of his ancestors looked like as displayed in the image before him. Lathering his face, he decided he looked pretty much as he always had, and the razor whisked its way through the first swath of lather. The cold water jolted him. Parting the curtains on the bathroom window, he saw that it was ten below. The sky was teeming with stars. Bundling up, he walked the hundred-plus yards to the cookhouse.

It was six in the morning. Half a dozen weather-beaten, alcohol-abused bodies sat quietly waiting for the cook to ring the bell for breakfast. This cook had been at the ranch for about six months. He prepared good food, but it was almost time for him to go to town. The thought of having to have another cook, even for a few weeks, was not an appetizing thought. He just hoped that whoever came back with him would not be so hungover that he couldn't work for a day or two after getting home. That would mean his having to cook for a couple of days; maybe it wouldn't be that bad, but only time would tell. The bell rang; the men shuffled into the dining room and began to fill their plates with hot food and cups of steaming coffee.

Breakfast didn't take long, and the men filed outside to smoke as they made their way to the bunkhouse to get ready for the day's work. He asked the cook when he wanted to go into town, and was surprised to find out that the day of departure had been postponed by a month. Cooks were difficult. Good cooks were the exception, and having discovered this man's talent, Willy made an effort to accommodate his peculiarities. He also gave him a raise, and upon hearing of his delayed departure told him he would be getting a bonus.

Treating the men fairly paid dividends. He had been able to keep the same crew for about a year, not counting trips to town. Trips to town consisted of going to the local whorehouse and then getting and staying as drunk as possible for as long as possible. He kept a supply of half pints to help the more seriously afflicted through the DTs. They appreciated his fairness, and when they came back from a visit to the whorehouse and a good drunk, they worked hard. Some of the men were good with equipment and some were not. He had a mechanic to fix the assorted rolling stock, but what he liked about the men who were good with the equipment was that they took an interest in keeping it running.

In the summer when it was time to put up the hay, he preferred to pick up the bales using the same antiquated piece of equipment his father had used rather than using the new machinery. Two men working steadily could do just as much, and more importantly, build a haystack in a straight line and tight enough to weather snow and the occasional cloudburst. By treating his men respectfully, turnover was minimal and work consistent.

Walking back to his house, he went by the corrals to see how his horses were doing. Their thick coats glistened against the winter chill as he fed them fresh hay and oats. It would be a long day, and a well-fed horse was a happy horse. He liked happy horses. His buckaroo rounded the barn and they discussed what had to be done. They made a plan, and agreed to meet in an hour.

Buckaroos, he felt, were like cooks. Good ones were hard to find. This one had a wife who took care of his house, and he had brought a decent horse with him even though a couple of the ranch horses were available for him to use. Dan was the man's name, and Dan got along well with horses. Dan and his wife Alice lived in a double-wide trailer that had been brought to the ranch for exactly that purpose. There was even a big satellite antenna set up and connected to the television residing in the trailer. He also made some of his books available to them, and because he valued their presence, they were paid well and given as much of the fresh beef as they needed when he slaughtered for the cookhouse.

Feeling the warmth of his house, he wondered how it was he had the attitude regarding the men who worked for him. He'd read about his great-great grandfather while doing research for his history thesis in the Bancroft Library at the University of California. He found that Simeon Wenban had not only been a very good mining engineer, he possessed the ability to engage with diverse groups of people and bring them to a like mind, usually his. But he also learned that Wenban had a way with diverse races as well. He was able to deal with the Indians in the area his silver mine was located. He also had Chinese mine workers, and the two groups coexisted peacefully.

It seemed natural to Willy that he, too, could get along with diverse groups. Where had this ability originated? He knew it was not a product of his own doing. This was the kernel that grew into a curiosity that would stay with him the rest of his life. It took him down many roads and produced many diverse results, both good and not so good. He saw Dan walking toward his house. They had a long day ahead of them and needed to work out the details of the plan they had made.

Coming home the other day, he had seen some cows and calves in the flat. The flat was a large area that began at the mustang corral, five miles north of the house, and terminated about ten miles north of the Walti ranch that was twenty miles to the north. Its width was determined by the Toyiabe Range to the west and the mountains on the east side (Simpson Range) of the valley, perhaps twenty miles across. It was a big area.

The cattle were not near the ranch end of the valley, but covering the ground to be sure none were missed and getting them into the Mustang field would take most of the day, especially if there were any young calves.

Dan came into the kitchen and clapped his hands to warm them, took off his jacket and hat, and followed Willy into the living room. They sat across from each other in the armchairs, and Dan said the cook was making sandwiches; water bags were in the truck as well as a thermos of coffee. They decided it would be best to split up after they left the Mustang corral with Dan following the Cowboy Rest road along the west side of the valley and Willy riding east of the main road, near the foothills. He'd sweep toward the windmill located about seven miles ahead and mark it as the center point where they would meet. Dan got up to go catch his horse and Willy followed him out the door with his dog bounding along beside him.

The old chute at the ranch had loaded thousands of head of cattle and untold number of horses; however, Molly's last husband thought he had a better idea and tore it down. Tearing down the old chute that had stood for decades was a metaphor for what Willy thought the man had been doing with the whole ranch. Dan had the

15

truck backed up to a loading ramp used to load tractors and other implements onto trucks. Every animal having to use the new chute balked and fought. The saddle horses were smart enough to quietly refuse. Using the ramp avoided any argument and made it easier for both horse and man. Horses were loaded; Dan, Willy, and Willy's dog got into the truck and headed off to face the day. Once on the county road, they paralleled a big meadow where cows and calves were moving toward the truck two of the men used to feed them. One drove and the other parceled out the bales in an orderly way so it all wouldn't be trampled underfoot and would give all the cattle a chance to eat. As they drove, he looked at the cows and their calves and inwardly gave Molly thanks for having bought that expensive bull.

They got to the end of the stockade fence and turned off the county road onto Cowboy Rest Road, crossed the almost frozen creek flowing down the flat, drove the few hundred yards to the corral, and backed the truck up to the chute. They unloaded their horses, checked their saddles, trotted up the field to the barbed wire gate, and swung it open. When they got the cattle within sight of the corral, one of them would gallop ahead and set the swing gate to close the cross fence and make a "wing," leading them into the field. This had been used to great effect when his father used to run mustangs. Willy called them feral horses.

Heading off in a northeasterly direction toward the foothills, he was glad to be alive, to be where he was, and doing what he was doing at that moment. He was grateful for whatever ancestors' genes happened to be dominant at that time. He looked across the vastness before him and felt entirely at home.

His eyes swept the sage looking for movement. Looking at the ground around him and in front served two purposes. One was to see if there were any fresh tracks, and the second was to see if he could find a projectile point. There was water flowing down from the mountains during the spring, and Indians had worked the area looking for game. He saw pieces of points, but not the whole point. The brush grew taller, and he headed into the arroyo and rode for several hundred yards looking for tracks. Finding none, he emerged from the arroyo and the tall sage and headed in a more northwesterly direction toward the windmill in the distance.

Ahead and to his right he saw patches of white moving toward the foothills. Smiling, he was happy to see that antelope stayed year-round. Off in the distance to his left, he could see Dan making his way across the alkali flat as he headed to the same windmill. Ahead of Dan he could see dust floating upward, and then reddish shapes with white faces. The cattle were opposite him and he quickened his gate to meet up with Dan and the cattle.

As he rode, he looked across the valley floor and let his eyes rest on the mountains. He could see where Cowboy Rest and Rosebush Canyon lay, and as the mass curved gently to the north the fingers of the barren foothills protruded onto the landscape, and the canyons he knew rose to the mountaintops. He could see Mt. Callahan and its snow-covered crater.

They met near the windmill. Dan had counted twenty-five head of cows, five of which were dry. He had pushed them toward the truck, and found the ten pairs he had farther north. The pairs would stay in the field, and the five dry cows would be taken to the ranch for a few days before a load of dry cows would be taken to the sale barn. All went well, and they headed home as the sun started to swing toward the horizon. Having the cows meant he'd have to use the pipe chute. Unloading had never been the problem.

Another Story within a Story

He had been unaware. He had been asleep. His life's complexity was well beyond his comprehension. Anyone looking at the circumstances of his life, anyone who did not know him, might have had just one reaction: Born with a silver spoon; he's got it made. Another reaction had been, and in the opinion of professionals he spoke with later in his life, one of wonder that he wasn't institutionalized or dead.

He had them all fooled.

His father's side came from Ireland, Scotland, and England, and his mother's from England. The Irish came into the United States through Boston and moved West, to California. Great-grandfather Thomas wrote and published a real estate journal, moving to San Francisco in the late 1870s. There he and his four sons became successful in real estate, and respected members of San Francisco's leaders.

The Englishman on his paternal grandmother's side was a mining engineer who came to the United States from Kent, England. His first stop was Cincinnati. There he met his bride, married her, and departed for the mining boom in California and Nevada. After spending time in Virginia City, he and some associates went into Central Nevada looking for prospective sites. They passed Mt. Tenabo, and Simeon Wenban explored the western slope, finding what looked like a promising vein of silver. His companions urged him to keep moving, as they were wary of the Indians in the area, having heard of war parties attacking settlers moving through the region.

Reaching Elko, he decided to leave his companions and headed back to Mt. Tenabo where he staked his claims. He set out for San Francisco to find investors. He was successful.

Wenban had a reputation for honesty and reliability that made raising money less difficult. He had the capacity to put people at ease, gain their trust. Not only did this work with Mr. W.R. Hearst, Sr., but with the Indians in the area of Crescent Valley. He gained their trust, and even though there were a couple of dustups, his operation moved forward.

Where would the railroads or the mines in the west be without Chinese laborers? Not only was there an Indian camp at Cortez, he employed Chinese miners who had a separate camp. The two cultures existed peacefully. In 1864 he sent for his family.

One of Simeon's daughters, Flora Wenban, kept a journal of the family's trip from Cincinnati to the mining camp at the foot of Mt. Tenabo. Her granddaughter, Mrs. Buzzy Mills, copied it and sent it to her cousin, Willy's grandmother, Flora Dean Hobart. It follows:

It was the spring of 1864 when Father sent for us to come to him in Nevada, and I think Mother's family (was) filled with dismay. The long stage journey through a wild country where Indians were frequently on the warpath gave ground for the most terrible apprehension. Mother had acquaintances in Council Bluff, and they asked her to come to them, and they would assist her in arranging for tickets and all matters needful for the journey.

So one morning we said goodbye to the dear grandparents who were heartbroken over our going. I shall never forget the day we came away. The dear old grandfather, so tall and straight with his fine patient face and his thick, gray hair shining in the sunlight. And the little grandmother, crying as though her heart would break, standing, holding to the post as though to keep from falling down. Poor dear grandmother never lived to hear of our safe arrival, as no letters reached them after we left Fort Kearney until late in the summer.

I don't remember the train travel. It was no novelty to us as Mother had several times made trips from Cleveland, Ohio, to Illinois, where her parents and two brothers had farm.

But the next day we were on a steamboat going up the Missouri river, and that was full of interest. The boat was much like the Oakland ferry boats in appearance. Inside there was a large saloon with dinner tables extending almost the full length (of the room), staterooms on each side with open transoms over the doors, and windows above them looking out on this upper deck where the officers had their staterooms.

I remember the windows particularly, because the (captain's) daughter and another little girl about my own age amused themselves walking on the upper deck and looking down through the windows into the passengers' staterooms. I had rather long hair, and it was being combed when they looked in on us and said, "Look at that girl's hair." I don't know how many days we were on the river, but outside the staterooms were plenty of chairs, and we sat there most of the time, as it was interesting to see the country. I remember a place where little frame houses were almost on the brink of the river, and as the waves washed the banks, a large quantity of ground fell away into the river and people exclaimed that it would soon take the houses away.

Among the passengers who sat there were ladies with their coloured maids sitting just behind them. I suppose they were slaves. One lady, who sat near us, when it was almost bedtime, took off her bracelets and handed them to the maid, but they both continued sitting there till it grew dark, when they both went to their staterooms near where they were sitting.

Mother found it was quite a mistake coming, as the proper place for starting west was Atchisons, and it caused some delay getting tickets and being listed on the Way Bill for the coach, as she wanted the entire backseat. But at last the tickets came, and we went to Omaha to take the stage to connect with the main road to the West.

It was almost dark when the coach started from the hotel where we had waited a long, dull afternoon, and it seemed very pleasant riding. And as we caught sight of the horses as we swung around the corners of the streets, we enjoyed the sensation of hurrying on our way.

After a while we became sleepy, and I remember waking up many times in the night to find that I was clutching the sleeves of an old soldier who sat just in front of me on the middle seat with one arm stretched along behind the broad leather band that supported the backs of those on the middle seats.

The next day we saw our first Indian. He was holding the bridle of a fine-looking black horse and standing
by the gate of a nice white house with lovely great trees
and a white picket fence. He had a light coloured blanket
wrapped 'round him and had a large black crow's wing
in his hand to fan himself, and the driver stopped the
coach and talked with him. The Indian shook hands with
all the passengers, even with my sister and me, calling
us papooses. The driver told us he was a Pawnee Indian
and that they were very proud and always carried these
wings to fan themselves in summer. He said that the
Pawnee tribe was quite friendly with white people.

I think it was another night and day before we
reached Fort Kearney, where we had to wait until we
were on the Way Bill of the regular overland stage.

The hotel was a log cabin with a porch in front, and
the people keeping it were very nice to us. Their daughter seemed quite taken with Mother and used to come
to our room and tell her of the young man from Wash-
ington, D.C., who was the private secretary to President
Lincoln and was on a vacation with a party to hunt buffalo and bear. We had bear meat for dinner one day and
I think we had buffalo several times.

Our last night at Fort Kearney was quite exciting.
Mother was getting us ready for bed when we heard a
great commotion in the next room, which happened to
be the dining room. She opened the door and found the
young daughter sitting half-dressed at the corner of a
table, crying and wringing her hands in great distress.
Her mother was trying to quiet her, but was herself
almost as agitated. They were saying 'We must go away,
we must, we must.' The father explained that the word

had come that the terrible Confederate outlaw Quant-
rill was near and would raid the place. They must seek
safety in Fort Leavenworth. After a little while, the girl
came out of her hysterical condition and her brother
came in bringing late telegraphic reports that were quite
reassuring, and it was decided to await further news in
the morning. Next day, Mother told us the rebel outlaw
was quite a distance away and not likely to come to such
an out of the way place.

At last we were on the Way Bill, but the coach was
not the easy riding kind we had from Omaha. It was
what they called a "mud wagon," and we were soon too
tired to notice much of the country, which seemed to be
an endless, grassy plain, treeless, and with almost no
living thing as far as we could see. Once we saw a large
gray wolf running along at a short distance from the
road. Paying absolutely no attention to us, it was quite
intent on its own affairs.

One day the driver pointed out a herd of buffaloes,
but at such a distance we could hardly distinguish what
they were. The poor creatures were hunted so mercilessly
that they kept as far away from the roadway as possible.
At another time we saw a number of antelopes racing
away, evidentially alarmed by the coach. We frequently
drove through funny villages of prairie dogs, and were
much amused seeing them sit up and look at us and then
suddenly flip down into the ground. Often a little gray
owl would be seen sitting with the little animals. There
being no trees, the owls made their homes in the burrows,
and we were told that often snakes were there as well.

We traveled day and night and made frequent stops
for fresh horses, and at irregular intervals we stopped for

food. We were given a room in which we washed and freshened up and had about an hour at each place. We sat at long tables that had benches along each side to sit on. Chairs were a luxury. The food was usually boiled beef and potatoes in their "jackets", and dessert was some sort of pie made of dried fruit with tea, coffee, and milk. Nearly all the stations were dreary looking places, the rooms papered with newspapers and with few comforts of any kind. It was an interesting break in the monotony when we had to cross the Platte River.

We left the coach and had to cross in very big wagons, with extremely broad tyres to keep them from sinking deeply into the treacherous sand that was constantly shifting in the river. The ford was wide and shallow, and after crossing we had to wait on the bank for the wagons bringing the mailbags and baggage over. I think Mother's trunk was the heaviest piece of luggage they carried, as it was made of very heavy thick leather, with wide, strong leather straps around it. It must have weighed all of one person's allowance.

A pretty little woman had come aboard the stage, and was going to join her husband at Fort Laramie. He was a captain so he had leave to come meet the stage a day before we reached Laramie. Mother had obligingly allowed the woman to share the backseat, so when the captain came aboard they took full possession, but kindly invited one of us children to sit with them.

Laramie was an exception to the majority of stations. The building was large and roomy and was very nicely furnished. After leaving Laramie, there were only men passengers traveling different places in the Rocky Mountains. I think it had been two or three days from

Laramie when we reached the station in the morning and found that the Indians had raided the place the evening before and had taken the horses and cattle. A man showed us an arrow he had taken from the back of a cow, which was in the corral. A telegram had been received, which said the station where we had changed horses late in the afternoon before had also been raided not long after we left, and all the horses had been driven off by the Indians. We had traveled all night between the hostile bands.

We had to go on with our tired horses, as that station was not able to accommodate passengers. When we reached the next station, we found everyone in great excitement, as the Indians had been there about sunset the evening before and had driven away all the horses. Some people traveling with their own team of mules had seen the Indians come down a low hill and capture their stock. The women stood wringing their hands and crying as we drove into the station. The soldiers had been called from the fort, and with men from the station, were on the Indians' trail. We couldn't go on, and Mother was terribly anxious, fearing another attack. The house was a long, low building, very comfortably furnished. There was a great square piano in the living room, and the family seemed very nice. We had breakfast, and Mother was given a bed to rest in. Her feet were so terribly swollen from not having sufficient exercise that she could hardly walk and they gave her a pair of soft slippers to wear. Sister and I were sent out to play in what they called the garden, though I don't remember anything growing there. There was a fountain built up of cement in the center of the yard with no water in it. A young fawn was in the garden, and after several attempts we succeeded in catching it. After we put had put our hands on it and had given it a few friendly pats, it followed us about all the time, even into the house. A high mud wall was built around the garden so we could not be seen from the outside and we were quite safe. It was great relief to run about and have exercise.

Late in the afternoon, we were startled by a scream and the crying of a woman. Mother rushed from the bed and hobbled as fast as she could to the outside door to see what was happening. She thought the Indians must be attacking again but found the woman crying from joy and excitement as the men who had gone out the night before with the troops of soldiers following the Indians' trail were now returning with the stolen animals. The station keeper's wife was standing with her arms around the neck of her little gray saddle horse, kissing and crying over him. He was decorated with a broad band of red cloth trimmed with long gray feathers fastened around his neck. The soldiers had surprised three or four Indians sitting with the horses in the hills and recaptured the animals.

After the horses had been fed and were somewhat rested, the coach was made ready and we started on our journey. We had to go quite slowly, and at every hill all the passengers except Mother had to get out and walk. It seemed to be the hilliest road we had ever traveled, but I think by night we were well out of danger, as not all the tribes had joined in the attack at that time.

It was a great event when a few days afterward we were told that the long line of clouds beyond us was really the Rocky Mountains. Even in the morning we didn't seem to be much nearer, and the views in the mountains were quite disappointing as we went. There were no vistas of interest until a day or two after when we began to see forests and could look long distances under the trees. We were told the reason there was no underbrush was because the Indians wouldn't let it grow, as it made for difficult hunting. The scenery grew more interesting, and one evening when we were changing horses Mother sent me for a cup of milk, and as I walked away from the coach I saw quite near a group of Elk standing under the trees, looking at the coach with great interest. It was a beautiful sight and almost made me forget my errand. I found the room where the men lived very attractive. It was just a small room built in one side of the barn. It was carpeted with big bearskins and had a variety of lovely skins hanging about the walls. A lighted lamp on the table made the place very cozy.

Most of the passengers were going to Denver or local places near there, and soon the coach was not so crowded. An old man and his wife came aboard a few days before we reached Salt Lake. The woman was very chatty but the man seemed in ill health and I don't think he spoke to anyone the entire time. He seemed to resent his wife's lack of attention to him. He snatched his handkerchief when she offered it to him, and at last she said, 'I've heard that when sick people are getting better they are always cross, so I think there's no need to worry.' She interested herself in the affairs of the stations where we stopped for food, and told Mother if they were Mormons, how many wives the man had, and if they were getting along happily. She used to get out at the steep hills and take Sister and me with her to walk behind the stage, and fill our pockets with stones she picked up, calling them 'transparent crystals.' Mother would quietly drop them out as we went along.

Salt Lake City interested us very much, especially the stream of water flowing beside the sidewalks. Young girls came out of the houses and would dip up a pitcherful and carry it in to be used in the cooking and drinking. The streams were only covered at the street crossings. I don't think there were any 'jaywalkers,' as the stream was too wide to step over and too deep to walk through.

After leaving Salt Lake City, there were only two or three passengers, and it became more tiresome than ever. We used to see beautiful lakes, looking so blue in the distance, but the driver told us it was not water at all, only alkali flats, which was discouraging. It was very unpleasant when we drove around long emigrant trains, as we always did when passing them. The odor from the brush troubled us so terribly. When we were nearing Ruby Valley station, the driver said to Mother, 'There is someone at the station who has been asking for you.' Of course she knew who that must be, and within a few miles of the station Father met the stage. After greeting Mother, he looked about for his children. Eva was sitting beside Mother so he knew her, but I was sitting on the middle seat with another little girl about the same age and he didn't know which one was his. He was so excited that he chose the other child as she was nearer Mother. Ruby Valley was a haven of rest. We had baths and stayed there two or three days. One afternoon while there, a terrific thunderstorm came up. We were interested in seeing a young Indian standing on the porch holding to one of the posts. With every frightful crash

of thunder, he would leap high in the air, seeming dread-
fully frightened.

The Indians in Nevada seemed friendly at that time.
We were amused when we crossed Reese River to be
told it was really a river. As we drove into it, the water
came only to the hub of the coach wheels. There was a
brook near Grandfather's place nearly as wide and with
as much water in it, and no one ever thought of calling
it a river. But several years after that, I saw it was about
half a mile wide; melting snow causing it to overflow
its banks.

Austin was another haven of rest, and we were there
two or three days. When we started for Cortez, we had a
light spring wagon with no top to it, nothing to lean back
against, and it was most tiresome. We stopped one night
with the Hawes family in Grass Valley, and the next day
our journey was almost intolerably long. We were all day
in the bright sun. No shade or cover to protect us, it was
the hardest day of all our travel.

Late in the day we arrived in Mill Canyon. We had
a log cabin and went to the company's boarding house
for meals. The next day being Sunday, many of the men
came to see us. I think they began coming soon after
breakfast. Sister and I were having our hair shampooed
by Father, and he would hold the dripping hair from our
faces and introduce us. These were men working in the
mines on the hills throughout the district and they were
anxious to see Father's family.

One unpleasant visitor came one evening when we
had been there a few weeks. We were sitting and chatting
with the mother and daughter of the only other family in
the district, when we noticed a mouse come out the other

side of the room. It acted so quietly, going forward and then back and then forward again in the strangest way, and presently we saw an immense rattlesnake coming out from behind a trunk going toward the mouse. Immediately we all began to scream, and Father and George Russell were coming toward the house. In the commotion the lights went out, and for a few moments we were in terror. However, it was soon killed. We had a bearskin of unusually large size on the floor, but it didn't quite reach to the front door. All the rest of the women were afraid to step without a light.

As winter came on, the Mill was closed down and many of the mines as well, and the places were deserted except for a few men who mined at Granite Springs. Father engaged a couple of his friends whom he had known a long time to stay with us for protection during the winter.

We asked Father how he came to find such a remote and out of the way place. I think his experience was the very interesting. He had been in the gold mines and was fortunate in finding a really good claim, which he worked with a partner for some time, and had visions of returning to 'the states' in another six months. But some unprincipled men, seeing his good fortune, came to him and said they were going to demand his claim as one belonging to them, and said they thought he was a 'good fellow,' so they would give him a sum of money to clear out and quietly let them have possession. He was very indignant and said that he and his partner had located the mine themselves, and they had no right to it. He would go to court about it. They said that would make no difference, as they could bring any number of men who would swear to anything they asked them to and that he was sure to lose the case, and that his partner would leave him to pay all costs and damage claimed, which was just what happened. After a year or two, he went to Virginia City where he had friends in the two Land brothers who owned a silver reduction plant where he worked until he learned the working of silver ore. Then he and another man formed a couple of prospecting companies and came to Austin and from there to Cortez. They traveled down Carico Lake to Mount Tenabo, but they located on Bullion Hill, where they remained during the first winter, the ores being packed into Austin to be milled. Austin also had the nearest post office.

There had never been any trouble with the Indians in Western Nevada, but there were occasionally unpleasant encounters with them individually. One day Father was riding alone to Austin, and stopping at a stream of water to let his little mule drink, he saw quite a group of Indians coming to him. He at once indicated his friendliness by giving them tobacco, which was the general custom when meeting Indians. One Indian put out his hand and grasped the bridle, and Father instantly drew his revolver and pressed the muzzle against the fellow's wrist. They looked for a moment into each other's eyes, and seeing strong determination in Father's eyes, the Indian let go of the bridle and stepped back, and Father went on his way. Another time when he was returning from Austin, he found a camp of some sixty Indians as he rode into Granite Springs. They came around him, and he supplied them liberally with tobacco and rode on to camp on Bullion Hill. The next day when writing in his tent, he saw quite a number of Indians wearing their bows and arrows in a rather suggestive way as they gathered together near the brush shelter, which was the cookhouse. One Indian went inside to talk to the woman, and of course she didn't understand a word he was saying, but she was trying to keep him from helping himself to sugar and anything else he seemed to fancy. She seemed terribly nervous, and there was no man near to protect her. Father strapped on his revolver and knife, and took the Indian by the shoulders and put him outside so forcibly that he would have fallen if he had not been remarkably agile. The Indian put his hand on his bow, and looking at Father, said, hanch (friend), and Father answered, yes, hanch, if you keep out. Of course, they only understood a word or two, but action speaks loudly sometimes. He gave them tobacco, and they sat down and had a smoke and a long earnest talk together.

The miners came for their noonday meal and took great notice of the Indians, particularly the leader who wore a necklace of bear claws. They called him Grizzly, and he seemed pleased with the attention. He was chief of the Tosse Wees, or White Knives, and came from north of the Humbolt River. The Tosse Wees were named from the spoon-like knives they used that were made of white flint, and they were the most warlike band of the Shoshone tribe.

Gravlley Ford was considered the most dangerous point on the emigrant route west of the Rocky Mountains. (Gravlley Ford is located two miles east of Beowawe and was the site of twenty-three emigrant killings during the 1850s and 1860s.) The miners worked in different places, only two or three in a place, and the Indians could easily have killed them all. They had come to gather pine nuts with their families, and the doubtless reckoned that the soldiers would come after them and they wouldn't be able to harvest pine nuts or fish in the Humbolt, and possibly they were impressed by the white man's courage, they, the Indians, became very friendly.

That winter, Father was ill with typhoid fever and stayed in Austin until spring. Later in the year, the camp was moved down to Mill Canyon, and it was not until then that Father decided to send for Mother to come. After the Mill was closed down, the place was very quiet and our only recreation was to climb the different mountains for long views of hills and valley, but never seeing animals or human beings till we returned. For amusement in the evenings, we had chess or cards or candy-making. One day, Father and several men went to the valley beyond the hills to look for cattle, as we needed fresh meat. As they neared the Wells, they saw two Indians come out of the window of a house where provisions were stored.

The Indians, seeing them, ran away some little distance and were not making much speed, so to show them they were not out of range Father fired his rifle, aiming well beyond them. This made them jump up, and they ran in leaps till well away. The men boarded up the window and went on into the valley. But when they returned later they found that the Indians had returned and had broken into the store room again and taken a tent and what provisions they could carry away. Sometime after that, a friendly Indian who worked bringing wood and water for us was sent down to the valley to bring in the saddle horses. He came back after an hour or two and seemed terribly alarmed. He had raced the horses up the canyon and said the Tosee Wees were on the warpath; he had seen the head of one behind a big boulder and he would not stay with us; it was too dangerous. He said if any Indians came up the canyon our men must all the time shoot. But the Indians coming down from the mountains would be friends.

Father had gone to San Francisco to buy out George Hearst's (Father of William Randolph Hearst) interest in the St. Louis mine, but the men prepared to defend the place even though they professed to being skeptical regarding any serious danger. Nothing happened, but later we heard that at Beowawe the stockmen had been attacked. Their cattle was driven away by the Indians, but the mules that had been used in Cortez were put in the corral, and one cow that had been in Cortez during the summer was not allowed to follow the other cattle but was carefully turned into the corral with the mules and left unharmed. The men were not hurt though they heard arrows flying over their heads as they secreted themselves in the willows along the river.

In Austin, there were wild rumors of an Indian attack on Cortez and the people were agitated by an account of Indians having killed sixteen men in the camp. A rescue party formed and came out to our place, which vexed my Father very much, as he said if they came hunting Indians they were likely to see some of our friendly tribe. Being excited, they might injure some of them and thereby cause the entire tribe to war on us. He assured the men there was no need for alarm and wrote a letter to the newspaper telling them how much their interest was appreciated but that we felt that we were in no danger, as the Indians in our neighborhood had given every evidence of a kindly feeling toward us. Our little camp was rather amused with the account in the papers, as there were only about sixteen persons all told in the place.

A few weeks after Father returned home from San Francisco, the Indian who had attached himself to us came to stay and built himself a little shelter in a ravine above our home. It was very cleverly arranged with rocks and cedar boughs, and no one would have thought it anything more than a part of a low growing tree. We never saw any firelight at night, and only in midday a little smoke would rise from it.

Late in the spring, he gave us news of the Tosee Wees. The soldiers had succeeded in dispersing them quite effectively and the chief, Grizzly, had only saved his life swimming long distance in the Humbolt River. One day in the summer, several Indians came to the house to ask if Father would be friends with Grizzly (his real name was Co-Youit, meaning great fighter). He was staying in the Indian camp and had sent to ask if Capitan Winn, as they called Father, would shake hands with him.

Of course he was invited to come and be friends. He brought a present of a number of fine large trout and wanted a pair of trousers and shirt, which was given him. Even after, he made yearly visits to see Capitan Winn, but he insisted that his name was not Grizzly anymore, but rather Capitan Pete.

Several years later, the smallpox broke out among the Tosee Wees, and Capitan Pete was on his way to Cortez when he was taken sick at Hot Springs. He died there.

The pine nut harvest was particularly good that year, and the Tosee Wees who succeeded in reaching a canyon beyond the wells were able to recover when they had pine nuts to eat. Some quality in the nuts affected a cure. But we were considerably alarmed when some of them came to the house bringing pine nuts to exchange for flour or beef. Mother would put down a pan for them to put the nuts in, and we didn't dare touch the nuts for fear of infection. We would take them away and bury them in the ground and use only the nuts brought by our own well known Indians, who were in a different part of the country and were as much afraid of the infection as we were. So many perished that the Tosee Wee band were never warlike again, and the railroad being built through the country ended the coming of the emigrant trains.

When Sister (Eva) and I went to California to enter school, we went to Austin by local stage, owned by George Russell. After a night in Austin, we took the overland stage to a station near Carson City and changed to another, which went to Winnemucca, and from there we went by rail to Sacramento. There were no sleeping cars, and we had traveled all night so were very glad of a few hours in the Golden Eagle Hotel to rest and wash away some of the dust of our stage ride.

Father had some business to attend to in Sacramento and had decided to go to San Francisco by boat, which was much pleasanter. We arrived in San Francisco the day after a very severe earthquake, and the reports we heard were most alarming. It was said that many houses had been destroyed and a tidal wave had swept most of the city into the bay. However, we went to the Cosmo-politan Hotel, and after most comforting baths, went to bed and knew nothing of the trembles during the night, though Father was awakened several times by their shaking and came to see if we were alarmed, finding us sleeping soundly each time.

It was not till about two weeks after we arrived at school that we felt an earthquake for the first time, and we took it so quietly that we were highly praised by the teachers. When Father and Mother came down to see us in the spring, the railroad was well through Nevada, and they boarded a train in Beowawe going to Battle Mountain. Staying there overnight, they took the regular passenger train to San Francisco, but there were no sleeping cars for some time after that. When we came home for our vacation in June, the passenger train made a short stop at Beowawe where there was only a telegraph office and a house for section men. Sister and I came home alone and Father met us at Beowawe. He had brought food with him and we sat on the bank of the river and enjoyed it, our first picnic.

Joe Dean

The image in Willy's illusion faded to be replaced by that of a large man with a shovel lunging at a smaller man with a pistol. There was a waterhole, and the smaller man, a sheep man, wanted to water his herd. Cattlemen versus sheep men had been a staple of Hollywood westerns for years, only this was not a western. The large man with the explosive temper and polarizing personality was a wealthy rancher. The sheep man wanted no confrontation, but he had a gun and found himself forced to use it. The result of the confrontation was the death of Joe Dean, Willy's great-grandfather.

Joe Dean worked hard and prospered. He raised Hereford cows and would go to the Texas Panhandle to buy the best purebred Hereford bulls he could find and then drive them home. He traded horses, a lot of horses. It was reported that just before his death Joe Dean delivered horses to the U.S. Cavalry and came home with $50,000 in gold. As the legend has it, that gold probably resides wherever it was he hid it. To his knowledge, Willy never heard about or read about anyone finding or claiming the gold Dean brought back to the Dean Ranch.

Joe Dean's daughters were Nevadans. At the time of their mother's journey to Nevada in 1864, Nevada was a territory, and by the time Caroline Wenban and her children, Eva and her sister, Flora, reached the mine, Nevada was a state. Their mother, Eva Wenban Dean, was a pioneer; so too were her daughters, Flora and Ethel Dean. Both graduated from Vassar in 1901 and 1903, respectively. Their maternal grandparents lived in a mining camp in San Francisco, on the corner of Pine and Jackson. Willy's grandmother, Flora, traveled to the Far East prior to the turn of the nineteenth century, and had a rooster tattooed on her left wrist. Her watch covered the tattoo. Her sister, Ethel, sat on the wing of a bi-plane as it flew over San Francisco Bay, and submerged beneath the ocean wearing a diver's suit and helmet, all while tethered to the ship by a rope and hose providing oxygen. Both were accomplished horsewomen. They were icons of San Francisco society in the early years of the Twentieth Century. They raised Willy.

He saw fleeting glimpses of his mother's family. His mother had told him that his maternal ancestors consisted of artists, businessmen, inventors, Episcopalian bishops, founders of New England, and maybe an alcoholic lurking in the bushes, but nothing that would shake the family tree. His maternal great-great-grandfather's family had invented the rotary printing press that revolutionized the newspaper industry. There was a famous portrait artist, a founder of the Grolier Club and owner of one of the world's most prominent book collections. He knew some of his father's relatives.

Dick Magee graduated from Princeton in 1928. He grew up on the Dean Ranch with Indians as playmates, sitters, and role models. Handsome, charismatic, an accomplished polo player, cowboy, and ranch hand, sophisticated, and intelligent, he was five days shy of forty when he married Molly. She was a maverick; a beautiful, smart, experienced, daring maverick, her own woman, and her own council. She had read the great authors, met some of them, and read them again. As a young girl, reading was her release into other worlds where she was never bored, put upon, or troubled by life's tribulations. However, the wheel of fortune turns for all, but not the same for all. Willy knew there were times she had felt crushed by the great wheel.

Molly Flagg Magee/Molly Flagg Knudtsen had had lots of articles written about her. She loved to have articles written. People wrote fascinating stories; stories she spun, and being a spinner of her own tales they all had good things to say about her. She also wrote articles and books about herself. Yes, she was that interesting, or maybe that manipulative. She controlled the situation by her command of the language, charisma, subtle body language, and eye contact to guide the writer's pen to pen what she wanted penned. An amazing ability she learned by listening to the people her mother and Harold gathered for parties.

To hear her speak about Harold Fowler, one might have thought he was running a boot camp on a Southampton estate. She told Willy that Harold was disappointed she was not a boy, so he simply treated her like one. Truth of the matter was that she was his disciple and absorbed the lessons as a dry sponge absorbs water. When Willy was nine, Molly took him to Southampton to visit her mother and Harold. Willy observed the joy with which they greeted one another and the mutual respect and love that carried their relationship.

An Elephant Hunter

"What's an Elephant Hunter?" Willy asked his good friend John Benson.

"Someone who shoots elephants, I suppose."

"No, someone called me an elephant hunter and wasn't very nice about it."

"Oh, maybe you're in the habit of chasing the so-called 'Big Deal, Big Trade' looking for the home run and easy money, yes. Well, my friend, you are an elephant hunter. You ever capture one?"

"Capture elephant, no; close a big business deal, yes, with help. Came close on several other occasions."

"Close is not closing the gate and capturing the elephant; that's wishful thinking."

When one really wants attention and approval from those who are absent, as in absent from one's life, bagging an elephant seems like a reasonable way to get their attention. The problem is too much posturing and predicting spoken too enthusiastically around people who really don't care: Parents. Their lack of caring hurt. That hurt is like a drug that makes one more animated and enthusiastic about what turns out to be a lost cause. The deal goes away. Approval goes away. Remorse and shame move in, and rationalizing victimization postulates why "they" are to blame for the roof falling in.

And on the occasion a deal does get done, there's no celebratory phone call from the parents or backslapping, because the ones one he wants to impress think he finally got it right this time. So, yes there is an elephant's graveyard. It's a lonely place.

However one wishes to define "elephant hunting," in this story, it is being defined by the emotional, psychological, and spiritual elephants one chooses to hunt. Willy might have been a spotter of big game, and he might have tracked the game, but having been trampled a few times he finally found it best to let other, more experienced hunters finish things off, and they did. To them goes the credit.

The other elephants in the room were more complicated and left no footprints, at least not on his body. Abandonment was the single most powerful force underlying the motives for most of what he did. It was a fear that was generational. What the word generational implies is that what gets passed along the genealogical tree has more to do than just height, weight, eye color, hair, and lastly, blood type.

How one has been parented influences the type of parent one becomes. If there are abandonment issues, whether or not a parent has physically or psychologically abandoned a child, the scars are real and have a real affect. There, too, are other maladies for which no one has given a truly adequate explanation, such as alcoholism.

Now, there's an elephant: Alcoholism.

The Funeral

"John, why don't you write down what you know about Willy, you know, a memoir, a biography of sorts?"

"Elliott, you are asking quite a bit, don't you think?"

"No. He was an interesting man, a man who did things in his life that were not the norm, and you seem to be the only friend of many friends who really knew his story."

Elliott Simpson had known John Benson since their days in prep school. They had remained friends through the years, and it was through John that Elliott had become a friend of Willy.

The limo stopped in front of the Episcopal Church. The day was dark, the temperature hovering in the 30s and a light snow was beginning to fall. The two men stepped out and walked in through the large, ornate front doors. They took off their coats and walked down the aisle and sat in the second row of pews, behind his family. John turned around and saw that the sanctuary had almost filled. He smiled inwardly and thought of his late friend and the circumstances that had brought the two of them together. The organ struck a note; the minister called the assembled to their feet, and the hymn "Once to Every Man and Nation" boomed throughout the church. The minister, a man who knew and had had lots of long conversations with Willy, began reading the Rite One

45

Liturgy. The recessional was "Amazing Grace." There were no bagpipers, but the organist was inspired and the music amazing.

The service ended and friends filed into a lovely room filled with flowers to greet one another. There was coffee, tea, and bottles of red and white wine. Cookies and sandwiches were passed. An hour or so went by, and people began to file out, leaving the two men to finish good-byes before they left too.

"Elliott, you've put a bug in my bonnet."

"Oh, what about?"

"About Willy. You've hit on something, and I have an idea about a small memoir. Did you ever see the memoir his grandmother wrote about Harold Fowler?"

"No."

"Well, it was short and to the point."

"John, are you capable of keeping anything short?"

"Elliott, would you be interested to see some of his writing?"

"I've read a couple of his books. Do you have unpublished writing of his?"

"Yes, you'd find it interesting."

The limo took them back to Willy's home. His family was already there, as were friends who had known his wife and sons for many years. There were two young grandchildren, a girl, and a boy. Willy loved his grandchildren, who scampered about and finally disappeared up the stairs to watch TV. Willy's widow greeted the two friends warmly, and they sat in a small group telling "Willy stories" as they laughed and cried.

Time passed quickly, and John thought for a while before he responded to Elliott's request for an account of Willy's observations on the human condition. "John, where do you suppose he came up with some of his ideas? On the surface they don't seem too preposterous, and given consideration they have some real validity. I you once told me he read many of Balzac's novels and short stories. Maybe those writings inspired him."

"Elliott," John replied, "did you ever get to know Molly, his mother? She was an unusual woman who, through the pages of all she read, acquired a worldview that was broad and accurate. Her experiences gave that worldview more than a bit of cynicism. She wasn't cynical, but some of her observations, as spoken to him, were. She thought some of the things she said in jest were quite humorous, but taken the wrong way they were so sharp as to inflict no pain until a leg fell away. You get the drift?"

John Began

Molly once said that her mother blamed her for the pain of childbirth, and childbearing was not something Molly anxiously anticipated however much she liked having sex. She read voraciously, adored her father, and from what she did not say, did not seem to have many childhood friends. Those she told him about he had met when he was in his teens in boarding school.

"He had a scrapbook of her as a young girl and was struck that there were no pictures of doll tea parties and the sort of girl things one might expect a mother to have when she was growing up. There were dogs and horses, and horse-drawn carts. She rode, she read, and she became determined to become her own woman. However, these plans were sidetracked along the way by the fact that her mother had the purse strings and occasionally would play the tune.

"There was a Frenchman with who she had been in love; she met him in England. The affair ended when her mother threatened to cut her off unless she came home, and home she came. Willy was perhaps ten or eleven when he heard the story. I remember he told me that his father was away and they were having dinner in the cook shack at the ranch. He thought it odd for several reasons, but was glad he wasn't French."

It became time for friends to say their good-byes, and the two men had gone to John's house to continue their conversation. Elliott shifted in his chair, then got up and walked across the room to the table holding the whiskey and ice.

"Can I get you anything while I'm up?"

"No. No thank you, I'm fine for now."

John stood, stretched his lanky frame, and chuckled inwardly as he thought of Willy telling him he was glad he wasn't French. Elliott sat down and sipped at his drink.

"What else did Willy say?"

"What? About not being French?"

"No, about his mother."

"Well, he said quite a bit. Some of it had to do before their reconciliation, and that was often times quite unpleasant."

"How do you go about defining that?"

"Well, as he once told me, his mother said that she and Lady Macbeth were sisters in that neither contained the milk of human kindness."

"Pretty damning statement, don't you think?"

Perhaps, it was she who said it, and there were others present who readily agreed with her. He said it was a statement of fact. He said he had once served at the altar and one Sunday, he was the crucifer, leading the clerical parade into church. As he kneeled to receive the host, he found himself praying for God to kill Molly. He said he realized that maybe he'd gone too far. And, Elliott, it turned out to have been a place where he began to discard his loathing.

Willy tried to put a bow around the whole thing, but the ribbon never seemed to be long enough. There were periods when he and his mother seemed to be on firm ground, and that might last from a few hours to a few months, but there was always some finitely small upset that wrought damage and long-term silence to their relationship. As he put it, they were 'very strong-willed, stubborn people, each wanting their own way.'

The truth of the matter was that they tried to recreate each other into the person they craved to have them be. Willy wanted a mother, and she wanted a genius, accomplished, well read, highly motivated son.

But as long as she used him as her personal tidy dumpster for all she imagined had gone wrong, and he dumped his fear and loathing on her, their situation was hopeless.

What happened to trigger these events and emotions happened long before Willy was born. His father was a vibrant, charismatic man who captured her heart, soul, and imagination. He was the rescuer she had long dreamed about, and he thought she was the wealthy maiden he had long sought. She sitting on the hood of his pickup and him standing alongside with his hat tipped back and magnetic grin, they looked, in an old photograph, like Marilyn Monroe and James Dean archetypes of everyman's and every woman's imagination, iconic symbols of love, lust, and satisfaction hanging in America's cafes."

Mummy Wounds,
Daddy Wounds

How does it feel to be blamed for the pain of child-birth? I don't know because I'm not a woman and I haven't had a kidney stone. What is it, what is it that infects and destroy a woman's maternal instinct to bond with her newborn? How does that instinctual bonding get ripped out of nature's process? What demon infests the soul at an early age that makes dolls and play houses and playmates undesirable? What message does that send a young girl about the role of a man in a woman's life? Can't be good.

What happens to a man when the father is missing, not involved, or too busy to care? Nothing good, I assure you. He tried to manufacture substitute mothers and fathers from all sorts of odd places and people. Regard-less of his intent, the result was always disastrous. He had only one father and one mother; however flawed he perceived them to be. He was stuck with them. He wanted to trade them in, and they seemed to want the same for him, a new model.

Dick had his wounds. They lay silently, unspoken unless he chose to disclose himself. When Dick was maybe ten or eleven, he was at the Grass Valley Ranch when, in a drunken outburst of rage, his father shot his mother's dog dead at her feet. His mother took him to the Dean Ranch and divorced his father, Walter Magee.

The Dean Ranch was fifty miles to the north. They went by horse and buggy.

As a young man in San Mateo, California, Dick saw a trolley run over a boy, severing the boy's leg. Dick crashed his motorcycle into a parked telephone truck, badly breaking both legs. His stepfather, Walter Hobart, treated him with disdain. Had it not been for the mentoring of his uncle, Fred Hussey, he never would have found a caring man or Princeton, class of 1928. Willy was told some of details these by his father, some by Molly.

Molly's mother divorced her father, Montague Flagg, because her mother attributed his violent outbursts to drunkenness. A brain tumor killed him soon after the divorce was final. Molly feared the whole thing was her fault and that her father's family wanted nothing to do with her. The list goes on. These and more Molly shared with Willy over the years. Unfortunately, none of this complexity translated into light, allowing that light to illuminate their relationship."

"John," Elliott began, "I know it's getting late, but I'd like to hear what it was Willy told you, you know, the ending."

"Elliott, it is late, not getting late, and for me to remember what he said will have to be put off, but I will say this. Willy said he had always blamed his mother for everything and anything that went haywire in his life. His anger and rage knew no limits. He acted this out in many self-destructive ways, but it wasn't until it dawned on him that he was railing against his father as well. Letting go of Dick was not difficult. They had moments of genuine closeness. Come by tomorrow and I'll tell you the rest of the story."

The Rest of the Story

After Willy was born, he and his mother resided at the Riverside Hotel in Reno. Reno seemed a better and safer place for an infant than the Grass Valley Ranch, two hundred miles to the east. Seems that Willy was a colicky baby, and his mother was not really prepared or willing to deal with an infant with a loud voice and projectile vomiting. His grandmother and her sister bundled him up and drove him to San Mateo, California. They took him to a doctor in San Francisco who did something to calm his insides, and there he remained. He said it was as if he had been enthroned in San Mateo. There was a nurse, cook-housekeeper, and a gardener named Manuel; they were his minions.

Although he had a photograph taken with his mother and father as an infant, his first recollection of them was as a three-year-old. His mother and dad had come from the ranch in Nevada to California to get some horses and take them back to Nevada. He was excited about seeing these mysterious people, his parents. They arrived in a truck with a stock rack. Inside the bed were a couple bales of hay and a sack of grain, and it smelled like horses and manure. He said that to him it was the best smell he ever smelled. There was also a puppy named Pedro. The picture seemed complete.

The truck had been backed into the drive of his great-aunt's house in San Mateo. There was an incline from the street into the yard that was bordered on the north by Acacia trees, the west by some citrus trees, a brick walk, three steps, and a walk leading to the back yard. The whole property was easily an acre.

He sat in silence seated next to his mother as the four adults had cocktails, and behaved himself with his best manners during dinner. Sometime after dinner, he said good-night and was hustled off to bed.

The next morning he bounded out of bed, got dressed, and hurried downstairs to find his mother and father. They were nowhere to be seen. He searched every room in the house including the powder room. He opened the front door and walked to the steps leading up from the drive. Nothing but silence greeted him. He glared at the spot where the truck had been parked, and in a fury, he promised himself that from that point on not a person on Earth would hurt him the way he felt at that moment. The cook came out and gently put her arm around his shoulder and led him into the kitchen for a hot breakfast.

"For the next five-plus decades he pretty well held up his end of his promise. That's not to say he didn't feel the sting of closeness; he did, but the sting penetrated only so far, not far enough. In that time he married twice, divorced once, and fathered two sons.

His relationship with his parents was truncated, and with his mother he felt a deep enmity. But as I have mentioned earlier, there were moments of tranquility and peace between them. He said that one of the high points of their relationship came when he flew her home, to the ranch, from Reno and landed in the 'yard'.

She had suggested that he land on the cricket field, a landing strip that had been built years before to accommodate tankers used to combat a plague of crickets. It was about 4,500 feet in length and paralleled the county road. At that point, the road ran along ground that was composed of gravel. It was smooth and firm. He had landed there before. It was about two miles from the ranch. His mother had him fly over the yard where the buildings and corrals were located, hoping to find someone around who would drive down to meet them. They did this about three times before Willy said he flew north for a bit, circled back to the south, and pointed the nose of the plane at the strip that ran from a stand of buck brush up to the corrals and ended between a corral and some parked equipment, maybe 3,000 if one ignored the buck brush and the truck.

The ranch was in a valley and the strip was at an altitude of 6,000 feet. It was summer, not too warm; the plane's fuel tank was two-thirds full, not too heavy. It was a Cessna 210 Turbo, which was good for getting out of short, high altitude dirt strips. Getting in was not a problem because the big wings provided lift and control. It was his first time landing on that short strip. His passenger was his mother. He was calm. Plop, no bounce, and a smooth rollout. Both were relieved. She bid him farewell and he turned around and he headed back to Reno.

Over the ensuing years there was heartache and turmoil, but throughout he thought if he just did the right thing, landed the big deal, stood on his head, she would become the mother he had always imagined a mother ought to be. Regardless of how hard he tried, she remained true to herself and chaos would reign. Their disagreements became more vitriolic and the silences between them longer. Then, one Sunday morning, Willy heard the pastor. What he heard resonated and he had a very deep 'ah–ha' moment. What he thought had been the cruelest cut became his greatest gift. 'No' became the pathway leading to the first steps of reconciliation."

* * *

"Remember those events in the lives of Dick and Molly I mentioned earlier?"

"Yes, why?"

"Willy said something to me shortly before he died about water running down hill."

"And?"

"And it's tied into what he had to say about remythologizing his life. Willy told me what he learned from the stories he'd heard and what he knew to be true about his family's history, is that long ago he had made a conscious decision that the buck would stop with him."

"Meaning?"

"Meaning that the family flaws he inherited would be mended on his watch. He said that he'd done his share of damage along the way, but that becoming aware of those flaws was one of the most important gifts he had ever received. He chuckled when he told me, and added that at least the brakes had been applied."

Elliott got up and went to the bathroom. John went into the kitchen and made some coffee. Coffee in hand, the two friends got back to the tale.

"John, why did I think there was a shared epiphany that opened Molly and Willy's eyes?"

"Because, Elliott, you only heard bits and pieces of what actually happened. The healing began a couple of years before she died. The schism in their relationship was not something that was going to just smooth over with a phone call telling her how grateful he was for her having turned him down. Thinking about all that Willy related about his mother's life, she was not going to suddenly forgive what had been said. There had been too many men who had let her down, and for some reason Willy turned out to be her whipping post. But he was the one who showed up when she needed a man to show up."

Elliott took a swallow of the hot coffee and looked around the room. There was dark paneling and old English painters mixed with Post-impressionists. Antique furniture was mingled with more contemporary leather chairs and a leather sofa. The windows faced west and east so the room had an abundance of light. The large windows were framed with old, elegant draperies that spoke of an older, more settled time. Off to the north wall was the requisite LCD HD television that seemed to be too big, but really wasn't. The TV was surrounded by a cabinet of bird's eye maple, bookshelves on either side. The speakers were at either end of the cabinet and the ceiling held several more. Underneath the TV was an assortment of audio equipment that could turn the room into a concert hall. But now, the room was quiet save for the two men talking.

"If I were to pick a starting point for two life-changing events that Willy experienced," John began, "they would have originated from the same source, the pastor. Pastor Jim. The man did not council Willy one-on-one, but his Sunday lessons held a truth Willy could not deny. Now, not everything the man said was absorbed and inwardly digested, but the words that mattered struck the mark. Willy, on more than one occasion, gave Pastor Jim credit for opening his eye to the message of Christ and the humanness of the Father. These were in place when the phone call that would chart his course was received.

Prior to that, he would call Molly once or twice a week and they would either have fifteen-minute conversations or fifteen-second conversations. She tired of him asking how she was, so when Baxter, her dog, got sick, her health ebbed and flowed with Baxter's. Then it was just as informative to inquire about Baxter. Her answer told him all he needed to know about her health.

In October of 2000, Willy was about to go out of town for a silent retreat at an Anglican Monastery. Before leaving, he called Molly and told her he would take her in spirit with him regardless of whether she happened to be a Deist, a Druid, or an Animist. She replied that she was 'an Episcopalian.'

In December Willy had a hip replaced. He called a week later to let her know all was well. He was surprised when he heard her say she had been worried about him.

Circumstance and Opportunity

It was early in March on a weekday morning that he received a call from a doctor informing him that Molly would have to be transported to a regular hospital from the rehab hospital. She needed to have a double transfusion. The doctor said her condition was serious. Willy thanked the doctor and called a man who had been Molly's doctor for fifty years as well as a very close friend of his. The man said, 'You had better come out.' Willy replied, 'Ed, I don't want to.' Ed repeated what he had said and told Willy he could stay with him and his wife, Tic, and where the key would be when he got to Reno. Willy called his wife and told her what was afoot. On the way home that afternoon, Willy called Molly's attorney, Gordon, who had Power of Attorney and was charged with signing off on any and all decisions that affected her. Willy had met Gordon years before, but had had no contact with him prior to that particular call. Little did either man know that they would form a solid trust and lasting friendship.

"John, what precipitated the trip to the rehab hospital in the first place?"

Molly was a slight but incredibly strong woman. She said, 'The body bent to the mind,' and about this she was serious. Perhaps a week prior, she had opened a wound on her left calf when she banged it against the corner of a cocktail table in her living room. Her housekeeper,

Yolanda, was there, and against Molly's considerable protests and in light of the fact that blood was pouring from the wound, called an ambulance. At the hospital, the doctor used a compression bandage that redirected the flow of blood into her leg and it swelled to several times normal size. At the same time, Molly abruptly quit swallowing. A feeding tube was put in. When she went home, a nurse's aide went with her to see if she could cope. By chance, Sally, Willy's wife, called to see how she was doing, and Molly handed the phone to the nurse, who told Sally that Molly could not cope and would be going to the rehab hospital. It was the last time Molly set foot in her house.

Molly did not think death was something she would have to deal with. As with other maladies and injuries that would have done in lesser men, she looked at death as something to be overcome. Only problem with that was it had only been done once before, and to her embarrassment she finally discovered that the man had to die first. She was not divine, but that did not stop her from trying.

She had a checkered relationship with God. Willy said that at one time, as previously mentioned, she had been very involved in the Episcopal Church in Austin, Nevada. When Willy decided he wanted to be baptized at age fifteen, she taught him the Catechism and gave first-hand accounts of what the Christian thing to do might be in several given situations.

But as the men in her life, the men she loved and counted upon, left her, she became angry with God. Job fascinated her. Maybe it was his faith that attracted her, or rather she identified with the disasters Satan had created for him. She stayed mad at God for a very long time.

Willy caught a late flight to Reno. She had returned to the rehab hospital after the transfusion. The hospital was on the way to Tic and Ed's. He stopped to see her. She was asleep, or pretended to be, and he left. The next morning he went to see her and discussed the several things he thought would be appropriate to accomplish for her wellbeing after getting out of the hospital. He asked for and was granted permission to speak with Gordon, her attorney, about the things he intended to do. Returning later that afternoon, he recounted what had been accomplished and what she needed to do. She peered known her nose, looked up, and looking him in the eye, said, 'Well, I see you've landed on your feet.' He pulled a chair next to her bed, and they began to speak about unconditional love and forgiveness. The next day he returned to Dallas.

Over the next four months, there were weekly trips to Reno. Sometimes Sally would go, sometimes both, but mostly Willy. He told me it was on the second trip to Reno that the transformation of their relationship became real. He went to the rehab hospital in the morning. There was someone visiting, and the three chatted for a few minutes. The two men left to go about the day's business. He didn't remember what the other man said as they walked into the cold April air, but Willy stopped and went back to Molly's room. She was occupied with a therapist. He asked if the two of them might be alone for just a few minutes. The therapist left. He sat next to his mother and told her a story about something that had happened a year earlier. As he finished his story, he said he realized that all his life he had blamed her for all that had gone wrong, and how wrong he had been. The finger of responsibility and accountability pointed not at the people he mentioned, but at himself. She looked at him with kindness and love. Gently smiling, she nodded her head up and down and softly whispered, 'Yes, I know.'

Mother and son saw one another as mother and son.

"What did he say when he told you?"

"Elliott, he said it was the just one of many steps along the road to reconciliation. There were a series of serendipities that took place over the next three months, each building upon the other that in the end bonded the two of them as if they had been bonded from the moment of birth. Quite an extraordinary thing when one stops to think about it. Also, there was another voice speaking to Willy about the things Molly wanted to hear. This would require him to cross bridges he never imagined existed, or ever wanted to cross.

"Elliott, remember he had gone on a retreat several months before his mother ended up in the hospital?"

"Yes."

He went on the retreat with a friend of forty years who had had some experience with a trans-medium named Geena. His friend treated him to a session. Willy said it was uncanny how she described things about him and others that only he knew. He said that some time after he came back from Reno, after the first trip, he called Geena made an appointment to speak with her. He also made the point, and quite firmly, that what took place with Molly during the second visit had nothing to do with any of the conversations he had had with Geena.

"You mean he was held spellbound by this woman?"

"No, quite the opposite. She did not tell him what to do."

"Then what did she do, say?"

She simply told him what she 'read.' Willy told me more than once that she never gave him a directive. From what he said, there were things happening that no one except God could have foreseen. He said Geena was a big help, but he was on his own as the situation changed. It was quite fluid. There were a number of synchronicities that he attributed to his faith and what he firmly believed to be the loving hand of the Holy Spirit.

"John, you've got to be kidding. Willy seemed to me to be the least spiritual person I ever knew."

"Sorry to disappoint you, Elliott, but from what I observed over the years it was quite the opposite."

"What do you mean?"

"I mean that somewhere along the line he became connected to a spiritual base that enabled him to get out of himself and truly put others first. On the two occasions he recalled, I believe he had to put aside his fear of having to confront Molly. He had to speak to her firmly and with deepest love and consideration. And on two occasions, he told me that the hand of the Holy Spirit empowered him to say what he had to say. So did a swift kick in the pants from Ed's wife, but I'll get to that."

"John, you mentioned something about many steps being taken. Would you expand that thought a bit?"

"Elliott, you have brought up something I might have overlooked. Willy began to stay in Molly's house. This was an important step because in the past when he had been in her home, either at the ranch or in Reno," he felt like a guest. This time he just moved in and got comfortable.

There were many books in the living room bookcase, and he randomly selected two that caught his eye. He said they looked like books she'd read for just for fun, so he read them. Being curious, he searched around and found poems she had written and letters written to her mother. I guess Molly found them after her mother had died. The reading of the books and poems and letters took maybe a month.

When he was staying at her house in Reno, his habit was to take an early morning walk, a mile or more, and meditate as he walked. As it was May, the mornings were crisp, not cold. One morning, as he walked, it dawned on him that the words Molly wrote might be the window to her soul. This he gleaned from all he had read. He knew at last who that funny little woman was.

When he arrived at the hospital, he went to her room. She was awake and alert. He said he walked to the side of her bed and looked into her eyes and asked her if the words she had written were the window to her soul. He continued, she nodded yes, and light beamed from her radiant eyes. I told her that I had just found the mother I had been seeking the past fifty-something years.' You know, Elliott, it was a special moment when he related that story. I can only—maybe I can't—imagine what it must have meant to the two of them.

The two men got up and walked outside. The chill night air felt good and cleared their minds. Silently, they walked around the block. Elliott said he wanted to pack it in for the night and John concurred. They agreed to continue the narrative the next evening. They would meet for dinner someplace where they could talk without interruption, probably in a casino restaurant. The two men went to the café adjacent to the casino, but far enough away that it suggested a quiet conversation could take place.

"Elliott, there's enough commotion in this place to start a small rebellion and nobody would notice. By the way have I told you what Ed's wife told Willy?"

"No, what was it that Ed's wife said to him?"

The Sun really Sets in the West

Willy and Gordon had had lunch and knew that the hospital she was in was about to boot her out because there was no more they could do for Molly. Willy said he'd explore a nursing home and report back. He did, and said it was one of the most depressing experiences he'd ever had. Then Gordon went and said the same thing. The good news was that it was clean and did not smell of yesterday's dinner. That being done, a date was chosen to move Molly to the nursing home. Sally, Willy's wife, planned to fly to Reno to see that Molly's transfer to the nursing home was made with Molly's comfort a priority.

The arrangements having been made, Willy went to visit his mother at the rehab hospital, and the nurse caring for her came and told him the nursing home would send her back to the hospital. 'Why?' he asked. The nurse told him that Molly had changed her code, back to Full Code from DNR (Do Not Resuscitate). A week earlier Gordon had arranged for Molly to change her code to DNR, but ever stubborn and denying death, she had changed her mind.

Hearing this, Willy swore under his breath and drove to see Ed to vent and get some advice. Sitting in the living room speaking with Ed, Willy said that maybe Gordon could reason with Molly. At that same moment, Tic walked by, and hearing Willy, turned and looked him in the eye and said, 'Willy, she is your mother. Talking to her about changing her code is your responsibility. You do it.'"

"Well, what happened?"

"Elliott, you'll be surprised to know that after much tossing and turning and a prayerful walk the following morning, Willy went to the hospital. Finding Molly alert, Willy sat on the bed, looked into her eyes and spoke the words that somehow formed in his mouth, and she quietly nodded yes. A nurse was called in and asked if this, changing her code to DNR, was something she wanted to do, and she nodded and mouthed the word yes. The nurse fetched a second nurse and the process was repeated with the same answer, yes. The barriers between Molly and Willy completely disintegrated. He said he held her hand; his eyes moistened, and he told her how brave she was and how much he loved her. She beamed.

The next week, Sally flew to Reno to be with Molly when she was transported to the nursing home. Maybe a week went by and Hospice was called, and a few days later, in a room overflowing with those who loved her, she quietly slipped away.

Death with Dignity

Elliott, Willy and I had an opportunity to discuss his feelings about the process he had the privilege to witness. One thing he was sure of was that his mother died knowing she had a son, and he knew beyond a sliver of a doubt that he had had a mother. He said that after so many years of trying to not be anything like her he ended up being 'Molly's son.' Yes, Molly really was Willy's mother. He went on to say the paradox was not lost on either of them. After all those years of trying to jam each other into odd-sized holes, each discovered the original compartments were just what they had been looking for.

Yes, Willy was also his father's son. Dick had been a more gentle man, a kinder soul than Molly. Once the dust had settled from one of their infrequent, but highly charged confrontations, Dick reached out to Willy and made amends. Willy told me that his father had once confided that he knew what it had been like to be treated as the bastard step-child. Dick's uncle, Fred Hussey, took him in tow and sent him to boarding school for a year and then to Princeton, class of 1928.

"Elliott, hindsight being what it is, think for a minute on the nature of Dick and Molly's lives. How do people, almost iconic, at least in Molly's mind, begin to find each other? Opportunity and circumstance found them at a

71

racetrack. She was having trouble loading a racehorse into a trailer. Up walks a man she has had dinner with once, who is charismatic, has a good sense of humor, and is well-educated who simply, and single-handedly, loads the horse into the trailer. In that moment the walls came down. The Justice of the Peace in Fallon, Nevada, married them."

"What Happened?"

"It died. They died. Dick died first. If ever there were two people who were given clear vision, loved as intensely and passionately as two people could, they simply failed to remythologize their lives. Maybe in the dimension they now reside that is what they are doing. Not a painless venture."

"John, how did Willy describe his father's death?"

"Lonely. Not lonely for Dick, but lonely and bitter and angry for himself. He said all that was the byproduct of omission."

"What didn't he do?"

"He left his father's bedside to pursue his own agenda. He behaved as had his father toward him. He simply left."

"John, why are you digressing?"

"I digress because to not bring Willy's father into this conversation would be like looking at a Monet with half of the canvas blank. But then some were—never mind! Those two were entwined within themselves and within their son. He could not have become the Willy we loved without their enormous influence and bold vision.

Through the sheer force, will, and personality, she had imprinted his mind and soul for both good and bad. He said that with one of his children he had the opportunity to walk in her shoes and experience what he had put her through. It had not been an enjoyable walk, made more difficult by the same template of intemperance and impatience as Willy had experienced. But, he added, removing the template allowed the same freedom to flow with his son as it had with his mother.

Over the five months of her ordeal, he knew where the road would lead. Molly was dying. At times he was impatient and asked God why she had to linger, to suffer, but he knew if he just kept quiet that the final jump would soon come. Her being comfortable was important to him. He had no choice but to go along with the doctors wanting to operate on this and that, but if he had had any say, he'd have told them to go to hell and stay there. 'Why can't the dying be left alone to die with dignity?' By alone, he meant no surgery on sick, feeble, and almost helpless patients.

Honor what's left of their lives. Honor the sick and suffering. Allow them to become the teachers they have become and need to be. Being in the room when a loved one dies is a privilege, not an obligation. Her being able to die with dignity was important for Willy, for Molly, and for her close friends who were in that room when she did die.

He used to badger the acute care hospital staff about Hospice. It was a useless effort, because hospitals don't want to kill off the patients that milk Medicare. They want to prop them up in chairs and pretend that physical therapy is helping. To show the patient is making progress. 'Oh, she's just fine, sitting up in a chair.' He saw her 'sitting up' one morning and she looked like a trussed turkey. She was strapped to the back of the chair with her head falling to one side. Drunks are treated with more dignity than dying, elderly patients.

In the nursing home, Hospice in place, he became a team player. There were lots of supporting members, but the care and understanding of the Hospice doctors, nurses, and social workers as well as nursing home staff stood in stark contrast to what had been experienced in other settings."

"John, what did he mean by 'team player'?"

"Willy told me he would call the Hospice chaplain when he came back into town after Molly died. He was worried that he had gone overboard telling the Hospice doctor about the pain she was experiencing. She had once kidded him he needed to be like the Trojan boy who put a fox under his tunic only to have the fox eat his innards. She refused to acknowledge pain. 'The mind controls the body.' She didn't appear to be in pain, but when asked by the Hospice doctor if she were in pain, Willy suggested the doctor reposition her arm. As the doctor began to move her arm, she winced. It was a big wince that jerked her whole body. Five minutes later she was receiving one-and-a half CCs of morphine every hour. She was no longer in pain. A few days later, the morphine stilled her breathing and her life quietly ended.

"The chaplain told him he had become part of the Hospice team that allowed them to do what they do, quiet the pain and ease the suffering, allowing the patient to die with dignity. Dr. Ed told him to 'think of it as doing something for Molly rather than doing something to her.'"

"John, is there anything else? Have you gotten it all?"

"Elliott, Willy told me something I think you'll find to be as much fun as he had telling me."

"What did he do?"

"He put the pelt from a bobcat head in her coffin. It was one she had shot."

LaVergne, TN USA
28 November 2010

206529LV00001B/19/P